MW01038889

Abby in Orbit

ALL SYSTEMS WHOA

Andrea J. Loney

illustrated by Fuuji Takashi

Albert Whitman & Company
Chicago, Illinois

To kids on the path to their dreams and to kids still finding their way. Enjoy the journey!—AJL

To my Lord, Jesus; may You be glorified—FT

Library of Congress Cataloging-in-Publication data is on file with the publisher.
Text copyright © 2023 by Andrea J. Loney
Illustrations copyright © 2023 by Albert Whitman & Company
Illustrations by Fuuji Takashi
First published in the United States of America in 2023 by Albert Whitman & Company
ISBN 978-0-8075-0095-8 (hardcover)
ISBN 978-0-8075-0096-5 (ebook)
Printed in the United States of America
10 9 8 7 6 5 4 3 2 1 CG 28 27 26 25 24 23

Design by Erin McMahon

For more information about Albert Whitman & Company,
visit our website at www.albertwhitman.com.

contents

Abby's Orbit

OASIS ISS

CHAPTER 1

Cosmic Critter Comforts

"Abby...Abby...*mira*..." Nico said.

Before I even turned around, I knew my little brother was talking in his sleep again. Nico loved bugging me, even in his dreams. His eyes were halfway open, little bubbles of drool floated from his mouth, and his arms stretched out in front of him like a zombie's.

Sleeping in microgravity on the OASIS International Space Station was eleventy-seventy kinds of weird.

I batted the drool bubbles away and tucked Nico's arms back into his sleeping bag. By the time I zipped up my own bag, he was snoring. Finally, I put in one earphone, snuggled into my bag with my tablet, and turned on my *Cosmic Critter Colony* game.

The bouncy theme music made me smile. My favorite little space creatures filled the screen.

At the start of each game, I chose a fun new outfit for my own charac-ter. Next, I planned huge parties for my happy little critters. Every time I greeted them, fed them, or gave them a gift, I'd hear a cute little *ba-da-ding!* chime that always made me grin.

I giggled when Mir the Mouse showed off the new hat I'd just gotten him and when Sally the Squid used all eight of her arms to gobble up the fish dish I'd made her. After I set up Tammi the Tardigrade's pool party, she gave me six thumbs up! Then she shouted, "See ya there, Water Bear!"

That made me snort-laugh out loud. Too loud.

"Abby?"

This time, it wasn't my brother. Mami stared at me with one eyebrow arched. I was in trouble again.

"You know better than this. No games before school." Mami reached under my sleep bonnet and plucked the earphone from my ear. Then she held out her hand.

"But, Mami, I just have two things left to do for Tammi's party and—"

"*Ahora mismo!*" Mami said in her *español*-means-business voice. So I handed her the tablet. No cupcakes or new hat for Tammi. No *ba-da-ding!* for me.

"Morning, Mami," Nico said with a yawn. She gave him a hug and a smoochy forehead kiss.

"Now," Mami said, "let's all find something to wear today."

I dug through my bag of clothes. "Everything here is dirty."

"Well, since the last supply shipment was delayed," Mami said, "we're all out of clean clothes. Everyone is, all over the OASIS."

"Mission Control is sending a shuttle up this afternoon," Papa said. "We should have new outfits, fresh food, and more goodies before we go to bed tonight."

Eventually I found a uniform that passed the sniff-and-stain test—not too smelly and not too dirty. Meanwhile, Nico floated by in his soccer uniform from our school back in Texas.

"No!" Mami turned to Papa. "Jeremiah, how did he even get that on this spaceship?"

Papa gave Mami a big shrug. Then he winked at me. I tried not to snicker.

"It's Career Day!" Nico replied. "This is going to be my work uniform when I'm an astrosoccer player."

Ugh, he was right: it was Career Day. I'd forgotten. Okay, that's not 100 percent true. As soon as I'd woken up, I had remembered. The thought gave me an icky feeling in my tummy. I was 25 percent ready to just stay home. But when your mom's an astronaut, an astrophysicist, and an astrobiologist, it's hard to fake being sick. So instead, I'd decided to play *Cosmic Critter Colony*—at least that way I could start the day with something fun.

"Oh, Nico," Mami said with a sigh. "It would be nice if someday *someone* joined the family business, right, *mi corazón?*"

Mami turned to me with a look. It reminded me why I didn't want to think about Career Day. There were over one hundred people on the OASIS ISS, and most of them seemed 200 percent sure that because I was the kid of two famous scientists, I was going to be a scientist too. Like I had no choice in the matter at all.

"I don't know, Mami," I said. "We'll see."

"Moon Drop," Papa said to me, "no one's expecting you to plan your whole life out by the third grade. If I'd done that, do you know where I'd be now? I'd be a professional LEGO model builder, a dog walker, and a running back for the Dallas Cowboys."

"Papa," Nico said as he changed his clothes again, "that would have been so cool."

Papa shrugged. "Maybe. But I wouldn't have met your mother or had you two or gone to the moon. It all worked out the way it was supposed to. So will your dreams, Abby. Just have fun today."

Papa's words made me feel 150 percent better.

"Okay." Nico floated by in nothing but underpants and mismatched socks. "I'm ready for Career Day!"

"Psst—son?" Papa tried not to laugh. "Your drawers

are showing."

"Nicodemus Alejandro Baxter!" Mami used all my brother's names. "You are not leaving this pod in your *calzoncillos*!"

"But they're clean!" Nico said.

Mami sighed. "I cannot wait until that supply shuttle gets here."

CHAPTER 2

Career Day Dilemma

The door to the OASIS ISS One Pod Schoolhouse *shuuushed* open. As soon as I saw the other kids and the flashing Welcome to Career Day holographic sign, I was ready to go home and crawl back into my sleeping bag.

"Cheese and craters," I moaned.

My schoolmates were 512 percent more ready for Career Day than I was. Some of the kids wore costumes, including space-walk helmets. Some of the bigger kids had brought their own work tools. And even though I wasn't the only kid with stains on my clothes, I felt like I was the only one who wasn't ready to start a whole new job on the OASIS before the first class bell rang.

When I joined Gracie Chen and Dmitry Petrov at our Level 2 station, Gracie was sketching different types of astronauts on her tablet. Dmitry was showing her an old scrap of fabric.

"What's that?" I asked.

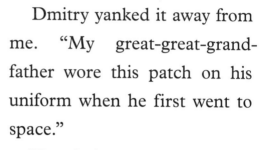

Dmitry yanked it away from me. "My great-great-grandfather wore this patch on his uniform when he first went to space."

"People from Dmitry's family have been going to space since way back in the 1960s," Gracie said. "That's almost one hundred years!"

"That is true." Dmitry's chest puffed up with pride. "My father, his uncles, his grandfather, his great-grandfather, and now, yours truly, Dmitry Petrov. It is our family tradition."

At that moment, I remembered what Mami

had said about the Baxter family business. I shook the thought out of my head.

"Are you okay, Abby?" Gracie asked. "You don't seem too excited about Career Day. Usually you're excited about everything."

"Well," I said, "you're awesome at drawing. And Dmitry's already planned a seat on a spaceship for himself, his future kids, and their future great-great-grandkids."

"That is true," Dmitry said with a nod.

"But me? I don't know what I want to do when I grow up. I don't even know what I'm good at."

"You're good at being exciting!" Gracie gave me a side hug. "And you're really good at being a friend."

Gracie's words made me feel 200 percent better.

"Maybe those are job skills for house cats," Dmitry said, "but not human adults."

Once again, Dmitry was 175 percent not helpful.

★   ★   ★

"OASIS Schoolhouse Explorers?" Mr. Krishna called, beckoning us all to the center of the pod. "Welcome to our very first OASIS ISS Career Day! Today, you will be learning about the many different careers here on the space station. Each class period, you will go to a new workstation to learn about the job at that workstation and help the adult crew members. At the end of the day, you will pick your favorite career and give

Welcome to
CAREER DAY!

us all a presentation."

"We have to choose one?" I asked. What if I didn't like any of the careers on the ship?

Mr. Krishna didn't seem to hear me. "Your tablet will show you directions to your assigned workstation for each class period."

"We have to go by ourselves?" Gracie asked.

"You'll be fine," said Mr. Krishna. "Just follow the map, listen, and learn."

Gracie gave Mr. Krishna a tiny nod, but she was still pretty nervous. I could tell by the way she looked down at her feet. I squeezed her hand. Gracie squeezed my hand back and smiled.

It was a little thing, but helping Gracie feel better made me feel better too. So what if I didn't know what I wanted to do when I grew up? For the first time since I'd gotten up that morning, I almost felt like my old smiley self again.

Then it hit me. What if I treated Career

Day like it was my *Cosmic Critter Colony* game? Every time I met a new grown-up at their job, I could pretend to try on their career as if I were trying on a costume for one of my critters' parties. It would be the perfect way to see what might work for me.

I turned on my tablet and started my first checklist.

1. Start a list of important things to do for Career Day

2. Have fun

3. Don't forget to check things off!

Ding ding ding! An alert showed up on my tablet.

ABBY BAXTER—REPORT TO DR. CHEN IN THE GREENS POD

What? My very first Career Day assignment was with Gracie's dad? Interstellar!

I looked at my list. Check, check, and check! I was off to a great start.

CHAPTER 3

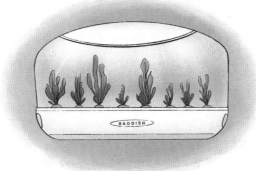

RADDISH

Meet Your Veggies

As the directions on my tablet guided me down corridors and through pod doors, I tried to imagine Gracie's dad's job in the Greens Pod. If we had been in *Cosmic Critter Colony*, we'd be dressed like old-timey farmers wearing muddy boots, overalls, and big floppy hats. We'd carry sturdy wooden baskets for the fruits and vegetables we'd pick.

As it turned out, the Greens Pod wasn't

green at all. It was *pink*. A soft, rosy light poured down on the racks and racks of green plants lining the walls. There were radishes, tomatoes, and some tiny scrubby plants along with the big leafy salad greens. There was even a row of pink flowers. The fresh, clean air of the pod filled my lungs and made me smile. For a moment, I even forgot about my stained and stinky uniform.

Dr. Chen popped up from a row of huge kale leaves. "Welcome to the Greens Pod, Abby."

He handed me some gloves and introduced me to his plants.

"Scientists have been growing vegetables on the space station for over fifty years now, but the technology has vastly improved from when we first started."

He showed me a spinach plant in a box surrounded by wires and sensors.

"Computers help us measure how the plants are doing, so we can give them each the exact

amounts of water, food, and light they need. Now vegetables that used to take months to grow can sprout up in just a few days."

Suddenly, my idea of wandering around like an old-fashioned Earth farmer seemed silly. Who knew that space farmers could be programmers, like my papa?

As I helped Dr. Chen pick radishes, peppers, and spinach, he told me about hydroponics and aeroponics, which were basically ways of growing plants without dirt. But the more he talked, the sleepier I got. After a while, I drifted off to the sound of his voice and the soothing music playing in the soft pink pod.

"Abby, are you snoring?"

"Me? Nope!" I shook myself awake. "I was just saying, I love this song."

"You do?" Dr. Chen asked. "I haven't been able to prove it scientifically, but I think it makes the plants happy. I know it makes me happy. I'll send it to you."

He grabbed his tablet and sent it to mine with a *ding*.

Just as I was about to thank Dr. Chen, an announcement blared through the ship:

OASIS ISS ALERT. INCOMING
DEEP SPACE CRAFT APPROACHING
THE PORT SIDE DOCK. ALL RECEIVING
CREW TO WORKSTATIONS.

"That is unexpected," Dr. Chen said with a frown. "The deep space pod shouldn't be here for two more days."

Dr. Chen quickly scooped our vegetables into a clear plastic bag. "I have to go."

"But our class period isn't over yet! Maybe I should go with you." I was 200 percent sure the new deep space pod would be more interesting than the snoozy Greens Pod.

"No, that's not necessary," he replied. "But before you visit your next Career Day workstation, would you please take these vegetables to the Cookhouse Pod?"

"Sure!" I grabbed the clear bag of veggies as Dr. Chen yanked off his rubber gloves and left.

Now *this* was exciting. I was going on an official Greens Pod mission! I opened the door and headed toward the Cookhouse Pod. But as I floated through the corridor, I heard a voice say, "Then we press this button and *bam*! The magic happens."

It was Papa! I followed the sound of his voice until I reached his 3D printing lab. Compared to the Greens Pod, Papa's lab was loud and bright. Nico and the rest of the little Level 1 kids bounced around the pod as Papa introduced them to 3D printing.

"Abby!" Nico shouted as he somersaulted over to me. "We're making stuff with Papa!"

Our father held up a glowing white bar. "We're making panels with luminous plastic for low-light conditions."

"Ooh," I told Papa. "You know what would be even cooler than bars?"

"What's that, Moon Drop?" Papa replied.

"Glow in the dark *stars*!" I said with a cheer.

Papa made some adjustments to the 3D model on his computer, and the printer spat out one star after another.

"This is interstellar!" I said.

I changed the design again to make them print faster. The stars flew from the printer. The little kids squealed with delight and chased them around.

Ding ding ding! Our tablets signaled the end of the class period.

"Time to go, Level 1 Explorers." Mr. Krishna dodged the swirl of stars and students as he came to take the little kids to their next workstation.

Then Mr. Krishna turned to me with a frown. "Abby, take a moment to consider the example you just set for your younger classmates."

Papa nodded and handed me a clear bag. "Yep, time to clean up what you 'starred.'"

I pretended to laugh at Papa's joke, but really I was 150 percent embarrassed by my own silliness. I'd meant to be mature, not messy. So as the Level 1 kids filed out, I took the plastic bag and filled it with the glowing stars. Then I turned on my tablet and went back to writing my notes:

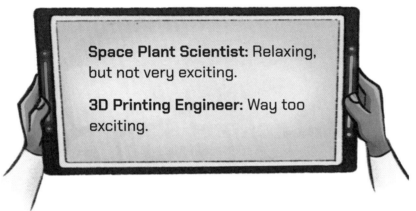

Space Plant Scientist: Relaxing, but not very exciting.

3D Printing Engineer: Way too exciting.

There was a third thing, but I couldn't remember it. And I almost forgot to check my tablet for my next assignment.

ABBY BAXTER—REPORT TO
MS. CHEN AT THE EXTRAVEHICULAR
ACTIVITY AIRLOCK

Interstellar! Now I was going on a space walk with Gracie's mom!

CHAPTER 4

The Cosmic Shuffle

I had huge plans for my time outside the space station. I'd just come up with a new dance called the Cosmic Shuffle—perfect for a space walk. It was going to be eleventy-seventy kinds of cool.

"Let's go, Abby." Ms. Chen pulled me into the airlock pod. "Are you ready?"

She pointed to the screens monitoring the top of the ship.

"It's showtime," I replied.

The next thing I knew, Ms. Chen was squeezing me into a space suit. Then another astronaut helped her slip into her own suit. Compared to our dirty old OASIS uniforms, the space-walk outfits felt fresh and clean. But they were also stiff, clunky, and hard to move in.

Nothing slowed Ms. Chen down, though. She gave me some more instructions, but I was so nervous I didn't hear everything. Also, by then, I thought I might have to pee.

"The most important thing," Ms. Chen said through the speakers in my helmet, "is to keep your eyes on me and listen to me. And to move when I tell you to move." Then she clipped us both to the safety tether that was supposed to keep us connected to the space station.

From the outside, the ship glowed white, almost like the luminous stars we'd made in Papa's shop. Then the light faded, and everything was black all around us. I could see the sun in the distance. The moon glowed above us. Below us, Earth shimmered with swirly, twirly clouds. I couldn't take my eyes off it.

So I spread my arms and whirled and twirled around, as Earth and the moon and the stars tumbled around me.

Then Ms. Chen tugged on the twisting tether between us.

"The show's over here, Abby," she said as she pointed farther ahead. "Let's get going."

We climbed the rails along the outside of the

ship like they were the monkey bars at school back on Earth. Ms. Chen found each handhold without even looking, like she'd memorized every single inch of the outside of the OASIS. I felt like a big, clumsy bumblebee bouncing beside her.

"We're making a small repair to the ship," Ms. Chen said as she pushed a large wrench into my hand.

She pointed to a bolt. "Go ahead and tighten it up."

It was easy enough to fix the bolt—a few turns and I was done. But in zero gravity, I could barely feel the wrench in my hand. Was it still there?

Craters! It wasn't. The wrench spiraled away from me.

"Hang on, Abby!" Ms. Chen floated away from me, reaching for the wrench.

Through the floppy gloves, I dug my fingers into the handhold, gripping it as tightly as I could. Then a terrifying thought suddenly hit me. What if the tether broke and I lost

hold of the ship? What if Ms. Chen and I ended up floating into space? My eyes blurred with tears.

"Abby!" Ms. Chen's voice sounded in my helmet again. "It's okay, I got it. We're all done."

Back inside, Mami and some other people helped us take off our suits and gave us sips of water.

"My little astronaut," Mami said with a big smile and shiny eyes. "When I was your age, I could only dream of doing a space walk. I didn't get there for another twenty years. But

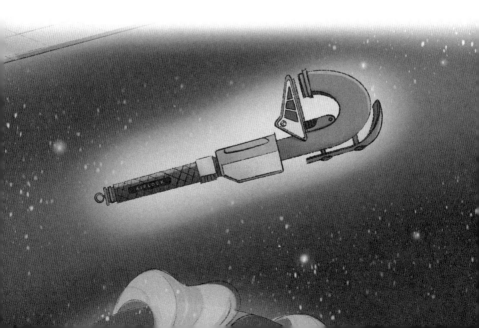

look at you, Abby! I am so proud of you, mi corazón."

"But I dropped the wrench and—"

"Watching you out there for the first time, Abby..." Mami's eyes glistened with tears. "It was like seeing your future right in front of me."

Mami gave me a big, squishy hug. I hugged her back. But I didn't tell her the truth. I saved that for my notes.

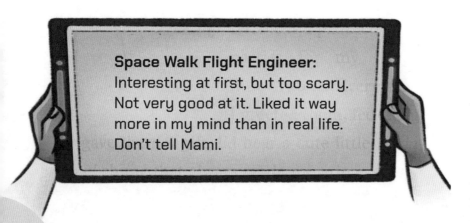

Space Walk Flight Engineer:
Interesting at first, but too scary. Not very good at it. Liked it way more in my mind than in real life. Don't tell Mami.

Ding, ding, ding!

ABBY BAXTER—REPORT TO MRS. QUINN IN ENVIRONMENTAL SYSTEMS ENGINEERING

Once I said goodbye to Mami and thanked Ms. Chen for being so patient with my dancing and my wrench-dropping, I zoomed out of that pod. Partly because I really had to pee, but also because I couldn't get Mami's shiny smile out of my head. The thought of me being an astronaut made her so happy. I wanted to see that same smile again, but for me just being *me* and not a little Dr. Silvia Baxter.

On top of that, I still couldn't remember the thing I forgot to do.

I had lots of problems I couldn't solve. But on my way to Mrs. Quinn's workstation, I found a bathroom. Whew! At least there was one problem I could solve right away.

"Ah, and we have another little Baxter."
Mrs. Quinn appeared next to the bathroom
before I could open the door. "Welcome
to the Environmental System Engineering
workstation."

"But this is the bathroom," I said. "And by
the way, I have to—"

I reached for the door, but Mrs. Quinn
pointed out the pipes and tubes snaking all
around us.

"The environmental system takes up the entire ship. It affects the air we breathe, the light we see, the—"

"Um," I said, still trying to hold it in, "I've really got to—"

"Oh, right," Mrs. Quinn said. "Time for the loo. But first, we'll need to fix it. The Level 1 children left things quite...untidy."

She opened the door to the bathroom.

"Cheese and craters!" I said.

Little handprints covered the surfaces. Disconnected tubes, used wipes, and little blobs of pee floated everywhere. It was 250 percent disgusting.

But I'd seen worse.

"This happens in our home pod all the time," I told her as I grabbed a wet wipe and swooped up all the gross stuff. "Nico's so little sometimes he pulls out the tubes by mistake and makes a big mess. Then I have to fix everything."

I quickly reconnected the different parts of

the toilet and threw away the dirty wipes.

"Wow," Mrs. Quinn said. "It looks like I'm working with a pro today."

I excused myself, shut the door, and made it just in time. Whew!

"Better?" Mrs. Quinn asked as I left the bathroom.

"Better," I replied.

"It always works out in the end, doesn't it, sweetie?" she said. "Now let's start the tour."

For the rest of the session, Mrs. Quinn showed me how all the systems of the ship worked together to keep us alive. They slurped up all the spit, sweat, tears, and pee that came from our bodies and converted that liquid into the oxygen we used for breathing and the water we used on the ship for cleaning, eating, and drinking. It was 75 percent fascinating, but at least 200 percent gross.

Ding ding ding! Time for my next adventure. Mrs. Quinn offered me some strawberry lemonade before I left. It was my third-favorite lemonade flavor after mango and peach. But I still said no. After her tour, I wasn't sure if I'd ever be thirsty again.

"Mm, mm, mm," she said, sipping the juice packet. "Tastes like teamwork."

That was 500 percent gross. To distract myself, I checked my tablet for my next stop.

TIME FOR LUNCH!

Ugh. Too soon.

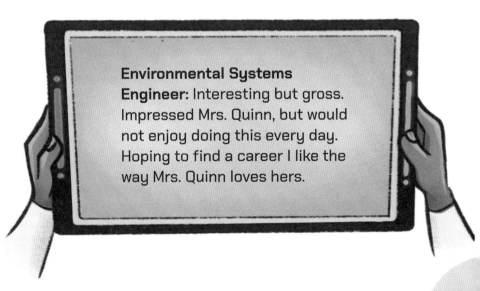

Environmental Systems Engineer: Interesting but gross. Impressed Mrs. Quinn, but would not enjoy doing this every day. Hoping to find a career I like the way Mrs. Quinn loves hers.

CHAPTER 5

Cranky Robots and Grumpy Grown-Ups

ABBY BAXTER—REPORT TO
MR. PETROV IN THE ROBOTICS
ENGINEERING STATION

After lunch, I headed to Dmitry's dad in
Robotics. The name made me think of the
old-timey herky-jerky robot dance that my dad
had learned as a kid back in Houston. I tried
a few moves, but they made it hard for me to

float through the corridor.

By the time I made it to his workstation, Mr. Petrov was already waiting by the door. He was not impressed by my dance routine.

"Sorry, Mr. Dmitry's Dad, I—"

"Excuses are tiresome." Mr. Petrov headed to his console. "We have work to do."

I floated over to him, waited, and listened. He explained that the robotics system helped the people on the space station do things that might be too hard or dangerous for humans.

"Machines like this are also useful for repetitive tasks," Mr. Petrov said. "Anything a person can do, a robot can do more efficiently."

I wasn't sure I believed that. Robots were

great, but they couldn't do *everything*. Robots couldn't make me laugh and smile the way my friends did. Or could they? What about my *Cosmic Critter Colony* game? My critters weren't machines, but they were programmed on a computer, just like robots. And they made me happy too. Wait—was Mr. Petrov right after all?

When I looked up, he was glaring at me again.

"Um, yes, Mr. Petrov?"

He sighed and looked down at the stain on his sleeve. Then he kept going.

"Today, we are using a robotic arm to secure the deep space pod that just arrived. The pod was programmed to attach to the ship by itself, but sometimes it needs a little extra help."

On his console, Mr. Petrov used two controllers: one to move the robotic arm around the ship and another to angle it so it could pick things up. Three screens above him showed what the robot arm was doing.

"Can I try it?" I asked.

"You can watch," Mr. Petrov said. "This is an expensive piece of equipment, not a child's toy. Wait—what is happening?"

Something went wrong. I couldn't tell what it was, but Mr. Petrov's face looked tight and angry.

"Mr. Petrov?"

He started grumbling as he used the controllers again.

"Is everything okay?"

"Nyet, nyet, *nyet*," Mr. Petrov growled at the screen.

I started to feel badly for Mr. Petrov. He looked stressed. His eyebrows looked stressed. Even his mustache looked stressed.

"Mr. Petrov?" I floated closer to him. "Are *you* okay?"

He leaned back from the console and crossed his arms.

"Well, Abby, since you asked...no."

This was unexpected. I leaned back and listened.

"First, I spilled tea on my last clean shirt this morning. Then your brother's class came in here and wanted to touch every single thing. Then some know-it-all middle schooler wanted to argue. And lunchtime? Ruined. They tried to tell me they ran out of my favorite dish, so I let that Cookhouse manager have it and—"

"There you are, Abby." Dr. Chen climbed into the pod, and Mr. Petrov grumbled and turned back to his console.

"Abby," Dr. Chen said, "our time together was cut short this morning. But there's exciting news in the deep space pod! I'd like you to see it. Unless Mr. Petrov prefers that you stay."

Mr. Petrov just grumbled and waved me away as he focused on working the robotic arm.

"Umm…" I floated toward the door. "Sorry you're having a bad day, Mr. Petrov."

In the corridor, Dr. Chen looked stressed.

"Abby, did you finish that task I gave you this morning?" he asked as we rushed to the Main Pod.

"Yes," I said right away. And then I thought about it. What task? What did I just say "yes" to?

Dr. Chen looked even angrier.

"I knew it," Dr. Chen said, mostly to himself. "I should go back to the Cookhouse Pod right now."

What was going on with the grown-ups? Why were they so mad at the Cookhouse Pod manager?

Then I remembered.

The veggies!

I was supposed to take the Greens Pod vegetables to the Cookhouse manager, but I had forgotten. I felt 250 percent guilty for telling Dr. Chen that I had done it. But where had I taken the veggies? I left the Greens Pod with

them, but where did I go after that?

"Abby?" Dr. Chen was far ahead of me.

"Coming!" I rushed after him.

I had to find that bag of vegetables.

CHAPTER 6

Deep Space Pod Party

While I followed Dr. Chen to the dock on the far side of the ship, I kept looking for the clear bag of greens. I didn't see it anywhere, though. Had someone else gotten them? I guess no one had taken them to the Cookhouse Pod if Dr. Chen was still angry about it. I wondered if I should tell him.

No, I had made this problem and I had to solve it. I just had to find the bag, get it to the

Cookhouse Pod, and ask the manager to make Mr. Petrov's lunch again. That would solve a bunch of problems right there. It would also solve the lying to Dr. Chen problem—although, technically, I only misspoke. Plus, if I could get the veggies back to the Cookhouse Pod, it wouldn't be 100 percent a lie…it would just be a time delay.

But I wasn't having any luck finding the bag of greens. And I didn't have time to think about the next workstation or what it would be like to be a deep space galactic explorer. I hoped the big news in the deep space pod would be about something exciting like aliens or deep space snacks.

Dr. Chen opened the door to the deep space pod. There were all sorts of buttons and tubes and wires everywhere.

"We're back, Dr. Vasquez," Dr. Chen said.

In a swirl of shiny black hair, a woman about Mami's age swooped over to greet us. And she was holding a plant, not an alien or some cool candy bars from Mars. Just a plant.

"She's here," Dr. Vasquez said. "It's a little Silvia!"

She took my chin in her hand.

"Oh, *mija*, you look just like your mother. How is she, anyway?"

"Well," I said, trying to wriggle my face out of her hand, "she's—"

"I haven't seen her since she had your *hermano* Nico!" Dr. Vasquez kept going, and the next thing I knew she was speaking in all Spanish. And super fast. I could pick out some of the words, like "father," "moon," "mother," and "work,"

but the rest went 500 percent too fast for me to understand. I'd hoped Dr. Chen would say something, but he was too busy looking at the plant.

Finally, Dr. Vasquez stopped and laughed.

"Enough about that," she said. "Today is your Career Day, so let me tell you about being a deep space astronaut. First of all, you have to stay flexible, because things can change quickly."

It turns out that Dr. Vasquez had come to the OASIS sooner than we expected her because something went wrong with her ship. It was better for her to get to us faster than to stay on schedule and maybe have more problems alone in space. She talked about the research she was doing. She even brought more plants to show us. Dr. Chen checked them over and pointed out lots of little details to me.

And wow, Dr. Vasquez loved to talk. Was it because she'd been alone in space for over a year? If I spent even one afternoon alone, I'd have a lot to say too.

But I had a plant problem of my own to solve. I had to find those missing veggies. I tried to sneak toward the door to the pod, but I bounced against some buttons on the console. When I tried to push away from the console, more buttons lit up. Then I tried to fix the buttons I'd pressed, but I couldn't tell what I'd already hit. Everything on the console was blinking and flashing. Worse, it looked like a countdown had started too. What had I done? I didn't even know how to tell them.

"Ahhh!"

A familiar scream came from the doorway. It was Mami. Had she seen what I'd done?

"Silvia!" Dr. Vasquez shouted from the other side of the pod.

"Aracely!" Mami shouted back. They gave each other a big hug. Whew—guess I wasn't in trouble after all. Maybe the countdown wasn't that serious?

"Silvia, I just met your daughter, and I know she's going to grow up to be a superstar like you."

Craters. Not the deep space lady too! Was there any place in the galaxy where I could just be me?

"Abby is coming along," Mami said to Dr. Vasquez. "And what's this I hear about your

new deep space vegetation?"

All three grown-ups talked about space plants and about sharing what they're learning on a video broadcast that would go to Earth, the moon, and all the way to Dr. Vasquez's station in deep space.

As they chatted, I checked the console again. No more flashing buttons. Whew! I backed toward the exit. Then I slipped out the door, zoomed down the corridor, and headed back into the Main Pod as fast as I could.

"Whoops!" I bumped into a grown-up.

"Watch where you're going, kid."

Something weird was happening in the Main Pod. It wasn't just the dingy, stinky clothes. A grouchy, gloomy mood had spread all over the ship. I noticed grown-ups scowling at each other, snapping at each other, and bickering. It was 300 percent not fun. I wanted to go back home to my sleeping quarters, curl up with my happy little *Cosmic Critter Colony* game, and try to forget about all the messiness.

Ding ding ding! It was time for my next workstation. I took out my tablet and went straight to the notes section to catch up before I forgot anything else.

Robotics Engineering: Kind of cool but mostly stressful. I wasn't good at it, and I didn't like it. Looks like it makes people grumpy.

Deep Space Astrobiologist: Too lonely. I would miss my friends.

All Careers: No jobs that make me a grumpy grown-up OR make me fix toilets all day.

I turned back to my Career Day workstation alert.

ABBY BAXTER—REPORT TO
MR. UDO IN THE ELECTRICAL
ENGINEERING POD

I didn't really know Mr. Udo, but I had a new plan. I'd check in with him first, excuse myself to the bathroom so I could find the veggies, deliver them, and come right back.

Easy, right? What could go wrong?

chapter 7

System Overload

Unfortunately, the gloominess of the Main Pod had spread to the Electrical Engineering workstation too. Mr. Udo, the electrical engineer, was in the very worst mood of all. Piles of messy wires and tools cluttered his workspace as he tried to scrub grubby little handprints from the surfaces of his console.

"Mr. Udo," I said with a gasp. "What happened?"

"Oh, Abby Baxter." He sighed. "The tiny children. Their little hands touch everything and leave this...stickiness. Why are they so sticky?"

I shrugged. Nico's sticky hands were a mystery to me too.

Mr. Udo pointed to the pile of wires. "When I was doing a demonstration, the older children wanted to experiment with the wiring, but they left before we could fix everything back. And Mr. Petrov—"

He sucked his teeth and shook his head.

"You don't have to tell me about Mr. Petrov," I said. "He was in a mood today."

"A terrible mood! He and I had some unpleasant words after lunch and—"

Mr. Udo waved the thought away with his hand. "It is too much for one day. But that is not even my biggest concern right now."

He turned back to the console and pointed to some monitors. "Right now, the problem is that something just started pulling power from the ship."

I floated over to his monitor, but I didn't understand what I was seeing. It was a bunch of numbers to me. What was pulling power from the ship? Gravity? Aliens?

"Whatever it is," Mr. Udo said, "it is slowing us down, which means—"

Commander Johansson came in and joined Mr. Udo at the console.

"Have you found the source?" Commander Johansson asked.

"Not yet," said Mr. Udo. "We're scanning the entire ship right now."

"If we are pulled out of orbit any further, the supply shuttle won't be able to connect," the commander said. "And you know what that means."

"No clean underpants!" I gasped. This was an emergency. Undies were at stake.

"It is almost as if the thrusters are activated

in the wrong direction." Mr. Udo pointed to a scan of the ship.

Suddenly, I remembered the buttons that I had pushed on the deep space pod. Had I messed up the whole space station? If I had, would that mess up the supply shuttle from Earth? What would happen if we couldn't get our supplies and our snacks and our underwear? And where did I put those veggies?

Now Mr. Udo and Commander Johansson were talking to Mission Control through the screen on the console. They tried to reassure everyone that they could still meet the shuttle on time. But I saw the little balls of sweat on their foreheads. That made me think of the water system, the fact that we'd end up drinking that sweat this week, and…again, where were those veggies?

I had to check my notes. If I could just retrace my steps through the day, maybe I could still

fix things. I pulled out my tablet. The power bar was blinking—how had it run out so fast? I checked my open programs and…craters! My *Cosmic Critter Colony* game was still running from that morning! No wonder I was out of power!

I needed a charger fast.

"There it is!" I found a weird old charger behind a pile of wires.

"No, Abby," Mr. Udo said, "don't touch—"

ZAP! All the lights went out.

Turns out, it wasn't a charger after all.

"Don't touch that rewired power supply." Even in the dark, Mr. Udo's voice sounded sad and tired.

The whole ship had gone dark. The sounds of people talking and shouting echoed everywhere. Fear grabbed my heart—was Nico okay? What about Mami and Papa?

"All sectors are reporting power outages," Commander Johansson said as she looked at her tablet. The screens over Mr. Udo's console had gone black.

"We need to let Mission Control know we've had an incident," Mr. Udo told Commander Johansson.

"I'll check and see if other units are functional," the commander replied. I couldn't see her, but I heard her leave the pod.

I could hear people shouting all the way in the Main Pod. I wondered if Gracie and Dmitry had already done their space walks. What if

Gracie and Ms. Chen were both stuck outside? What if Dmitry had tried to go by himself and gotten stuck out there alone? Each thought was scarier than the last one.

I wished I'd never left my sleeping quarters. I wished I'd just told Mami I was sick and stayed home to play my game alone. I'd ruined everything. Everyone was about to find out that I was the worst Baxter ever. Hot tears bubbled from my eyes and into my hands.

"Don't worry, Abby Baxter," Mr. Udo said into the darkness. "At least my workstation looks better now."

I laughed. We both

laughed. Mr. Udo's words reminded me of my father's silly puns. Papa always found a way to make things better. So did Mami, in her own way. And Nico made everyone laugh too.

Now maybe it was my turn to step up as a Baxter and make things brighter. For the sake of the OASIS ISS, the shuttle from Earth, and even the ships beyond the solar system, I had to fix this. I couldn't rewire the electrical system for the OASIS. But I knew for sure that I could do something.

Because I finally remembered where I'd put those vegetables!

CHAPTER 8

People First, Then Things

After I convinced Mr. Udo I'd come right back, I pushed my way through the dark corridors. I couldn't believe that this had all started with a bag of veggies. If I could find them and get them where they belonged, maybe I could fix everything.

Then something made me freeze—the sound of someone crying. The sound of *Gracie* crying.

"Gracie!" I shouted.

Using the hand-over-hand technique I had learned from Ms. Chen on our space walk, I pulled myself across the corridors, still calling for Gracie.

"Abby?" Gracie whimpered. "Abby, over here."

I finally found her, curled up alone against a wall. We gave each other the biggest hug.

"I was drawing one of the air vents," Gracie said. "And suddenly I couldn't see anything. I was so scared I didn't know what to do."

Then I remembered—her father had given me that music! My tablet had just enough power to play the soothing songs from the Greens Pod.

"Better?" I asked her.

"A little." Gracie grinned.

Gracie and I headed back down the dark corridors and through open pod doors until we got to Papa's 3D printing lab.

"Papa! Papa, where are you?"

He wasn't there, but something else was: a big bright bag of luminous stars! With the lights out, they glowed like the moon.

"Ooh," Gracie said. "These should help."

We took the bag and raced back to the Electrical Engineering station, handing out glow-in-the-dark stars to people as we passed. At his workstation, Mr. Udo and Papa were fixing wires and trying to get systems back online. When we showed up with the bag of glowing stars, I could see Mr. Udo's wide smile through the faint light.

"Abby Baxter," Mr. Udo said, "you are a constant source of surprises."

After giving Papa a hug, I placed glowing stars around Mr. Udo's workspace, and Gracie held Mr. Udo's light stick steady so he could

use both hands to fix the wiring. Dr. Chen's soothing plant music calmed all of us down.

"Very nice," Mr. Udo said. "Relaxing. I think we are almost done."

Finally, the lights blinked back on. All sorts of machines in the pod whirred and beeped back to life. People cheered all throughout the ship. We cheered too.

Mr. Udo took one glow-in-the-dark star and popped it into his pocket.

"I will save this as a reminder of you, Abby Baxter," he said.

"You just keep finding new ways to shine, Moon Drop," Papa said with a grin.

Then Gracie and I rushed to find her mom and Dmitry too, since we heard that he'd been on his space walk when the lights went out. When we got there, Mami and some other adults had gotten them down from the top of the ship. Gracie flew straight to Ms. Chen and hugged her. Dmitry looked shaky and wobbly, but Ms. Chen patted him on the back.

"It was a shock when we lost contact with the ship," Ms. Chen said, "but young Mr. Petrov behaved like a true professional."

"I almost puked in my helmet," Dmitry whispered to Gracie and me. "And now I have no more clean underwear."

Gracie and I giggled and gave him a hug.

"We're so happy you're okay," I said. I really meant it, even if he was a little stinky.

Then I headed for the door.

"Abby," Mami said, "where are you going?"

"To finish what I started," I said.

I opened the bag of stars. At the very bottom was the bag of veggies. That's where I'd left them that morning—back in Papa's lab!

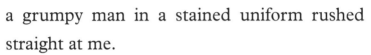

★ ★ ★

When I finally got to the Cookhouse Pod, a grumpy man in a stained uniform rushed straight at me.

"Hi, I'm Abby B—"

"I know who you are," he said. "You're the kid who started all this mess!"

"I'm really sorry." I handed him the vegetables.

"Sorry?! Do you know how much trouble you caused?"

"Come now, husband," Mrs. Quinn said as she floated over, "she made one wee mistake. Well, a few mistakes."

As Mr. Quinn stormed back into the Cookhouse, Mrs. Quinn cheerfully explained what had happened. It turns out that between me accidentally turning on the booster to the deep space pod and Mr. Petrov accidentally switching the angle of that spacecraft with his robotics, we'd slowed down the whole OASIS ISS!

"But we found the problem, we fixed it, and in a few hours we'll all have clean knickers and socks again! It all works out in the end, doesn't it?"

Mrs. Quinn's words made me feel 150 percent better.

"Well, almost," she continued. "You know what you need to do now, sweetie."

I did. I took a deep breath and headed back to the Main Pod.

CHAPTER 9

Cosmic Community Celebration

I spent the next class period apologizing to everybody for my carelessness. And I mean everybody: Dr. Chen, Mr. Udo, Commander Johansson, Mr. Quinn, Dr. Vasquez, both of my parents, the Level 1 kids, everyone who didn't get their greens for lunch, and so on. I apologized for not telling the truth all the way and not speaking up sooner. I even stretched out my tablet and showed how it had all happened, step-by-step.

As I talked about what I'd done, I realized that I wasn't the only one who'd made mistakes that day. Some grown-ups realized that they'd had a part in it too. The crowd of people watching my apology presentation grew larger and larger.

Then Mr. Quinn showed up with a special spicy veggie dish for everyone. Mr. Petrov went right up to him.

"My apologies, Quinn," Mr. Petrov said. "You are a good man who did nothing wrong. You did not deserve my anger today. I am sorry."

"I told you I didn't forget." Mr. Quinn handed a steaming packet of veggies and a fork to Mr. Petrov. "I even made it extra spicy just for you, Petrov."

Then Mr. Petrov did something I'd never seen him do before. He smiled! Then he turned to Mr. Udo.

"My apologies to you too, Mr. Udo," Mr. Petrov said. "My behavior has been beastly today. And to you, Abby, and you, Dr. Chen, and...anyone else?"

Half the crowd raised their hands.

Dr. Chen apologized to Mr. Quinn for not delivering the veggies himself. More grown-ups I didn't even know apologized to each other. How could one lost bag of vegetables lead to so many apologies?

Mr. Krishna patted me on the shoulder. "That was an impressive report, Abby. Well thought-out and detailed."

"Thanks, Mr. Krishna." I checked my tablet.

"So, where's my next workstation?"

The entire crowd hushed and stared at me.

"Oh, I think you've done enough," Mr. Krishna said. "No more Career Day for you, Abby."

I'm pretty sure I heard the whole Main Pod sigh in relief.

By the time the supply shuttle from Earth docked to the OASIS later that day, our whole ship sparkled and shined inside. Mr. Krishna had put all of us students to work cleaning and fixing everything we'd touched all day. The sticky handprints, tangled wires, and floating messes had all been dealt with, and nothing but clean and shiny surfaces remained. Like Mrs. Quinn had said, it all worked out in the end.

A few hours later, I was back in the Main Pod, wearing fresh clean clothes and snacking

on sweet, juicy mango slices. To make amends to Mr. Quinn, I'd volunteered to hand out extra goodies from the shuttle shipment. It was eleventy-seven kinds of fun. Grown-ups who had been so grumpy earlier in the day were all smiles and laughs when we handed out fresh fruit, tasty snacks, extra socks, and leftover luminous stars. I even showed some folks how to do the Cosmic Shuffle! Chatting with my friends, neighbors, and classmates on the OASIS made me feel like myself again.

"Once again, Abby," Commander Johansson

said after I handed her a lingonberry squeezie, "I'm impressed by how you solved a challenging situation using your people skills. Especially how you noticed the needs of each crew member today. You made them feel seen and heard. That's an important leadership skill."

"Thank you, Commander Johansson," I said, "I just tried to do what was right. Well, I mean, after I did everything wrong first, but—"

"We are so proud of her," Mami said as she and Papa put their arms around me. Even Nico hugged me, with his hands still sticky from real orange slices.

"You should be," Dr. Vasquez said. "She is an original."

I leaned into Mami's arms. She looked down with her bright smile and shiny eyes, and in that moment I was so happy to be there. And I was so happy to be me.

All through Career Day, folks had wondered what kind of scientist I wanted to be. That used to be my least favorite question, but now I wasn't afraid to tell the truth. I wasn't afraid to say that even though plants and ships and robots and computers were cool, they weren't nearly as interesting to me as what's in people's hearts. That's what really fascinated me.

So even though I made mistakes sometimes, I wasn't a bad Baxter after all.

I was just an awesome Abby.

"It's been a long day," Mami said. "You want to go back home so you can relax and play your *Cosmic Critter Colony* game? I hear Tammi the Tardigrade is having a party."

How could I leave when the Main Pod was filled with happy people eating, drinking, and laughing?

"Let's stay a little longer," I told Mami.

Then I handed out some more treats and danced with my friends.

Abby's Vocabulary

ahora mismo: Spanish for "right now"

calzoncillos: Spanish for "underwear"

español: Spanish for "Spanish"

hermano: Spanish for "brother"

knickers: British English for "underwear"

loo: British English for "toilet"

mi corazón: Spanish for "my heart" or "my sweetheart"

mija: Spanish term of affection for a little girl

mira: Spanish for "look"

nyet: Russian for "no"

Abby's Orbital Observations
(Real Science for Kids Way Back in the 2020s)

How do people sleep on the ISS?
Each astronaut sleeps in a small area containing their sleeping bag, computer, and personal items. Sleeping bags are strapped to the walls so that the astronauts don't float around. Because there are so many machines running on the ISS, it can be noisy. Some astronauts use eye masks and earplugs while they rest.

How do clothes, food, and supplies get to the ISS?
There isn't much extra storage space on the International Space Station, and there are no washing machines on board. Astronauts wear the same clothes over and over until they have to throw them away. Supply shuttles regularly bring more clean clothing, as well as food, medicines, scientific experiments, spare parts, and more.

What happens to all the clothes, empty food packets, and other trash the astronauts throw away?
The trash gets packed into a disposable capsule that is sent back down to burn up in Earth's atmosphere.

Award-winning author **Andrea J. Loney** grew up in a small town in New Jersey. After receiving her MFA from New York University, she joined a traveling circus, then stayed in Hollywood to make movies. Now Andrea teaches computer classes at a community college while living in Los Angeles with her family and their embarrassingly spoiled pets. Learn more at andreajloney.com.

Once a professional nurse, **Fuuji Takashi** is now a children's book illustrator and character designer from General Santos, Philippines. She is best known for illustrating Kailyn Lowry's first children's book, *Love Is Bubblegum*, and for her work on children's books featuring diverse characters. In her spare time, she likes singing, cooking, and taking long, peaceful walks.